So I guess you tapped the Hulk...

By Calliope Glass

Illustrated by Ron Lim and Richard Isanove

SHAKE TO ASSEMBLE

MARVEL

LOS ANGELES
NEW YORK

Printed in Malaysia
First Edition, March 2015
10 9 8 7 6 5 4 3 2 1
H106-9333-5-15002
ISBN 978-1-4231-7826-2
Library of Congress
Control Number: 2014944503

Published by Marvel Press,
an imprint of Disney Book Group.

For information address Marvel Press, 125 West End Avenue, New York, New York 10023.

Designed by Jennifer Redding

MARVEL
marvelkids.com

LOOK!

It's HAWKEYE!
He's one of the Avengers.
Let's assemble
the rest of the team.

TAP Hawkeye's bow once
to help him shoot the arrow.

Not bad!
Now try SHAKING the book
from left to right three times.
Maybe we can find
another Avenger.

Sorry about that, Hawkeye!
But look what we found—
THOR'S hammer!
With all this shaking,
it feels like a thunderstorm
is coming.

SWING his hammer
by moving the book around
in a counterclockwise circle.
Then **CLAP** your hands twice
to bring the thunder god
into action.

You did it!
Let's help Thor
clean up the storm.

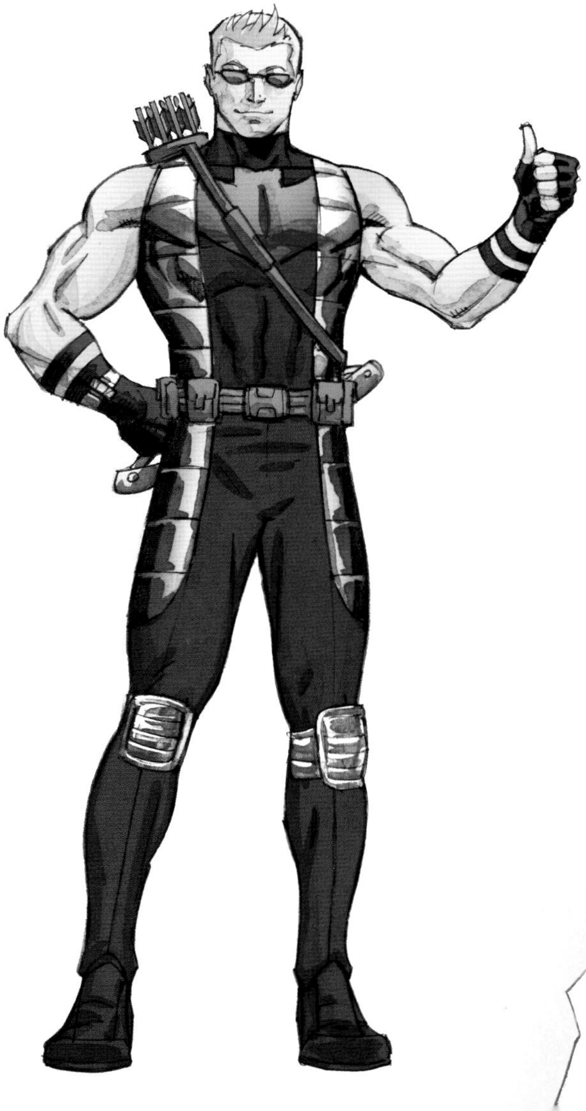

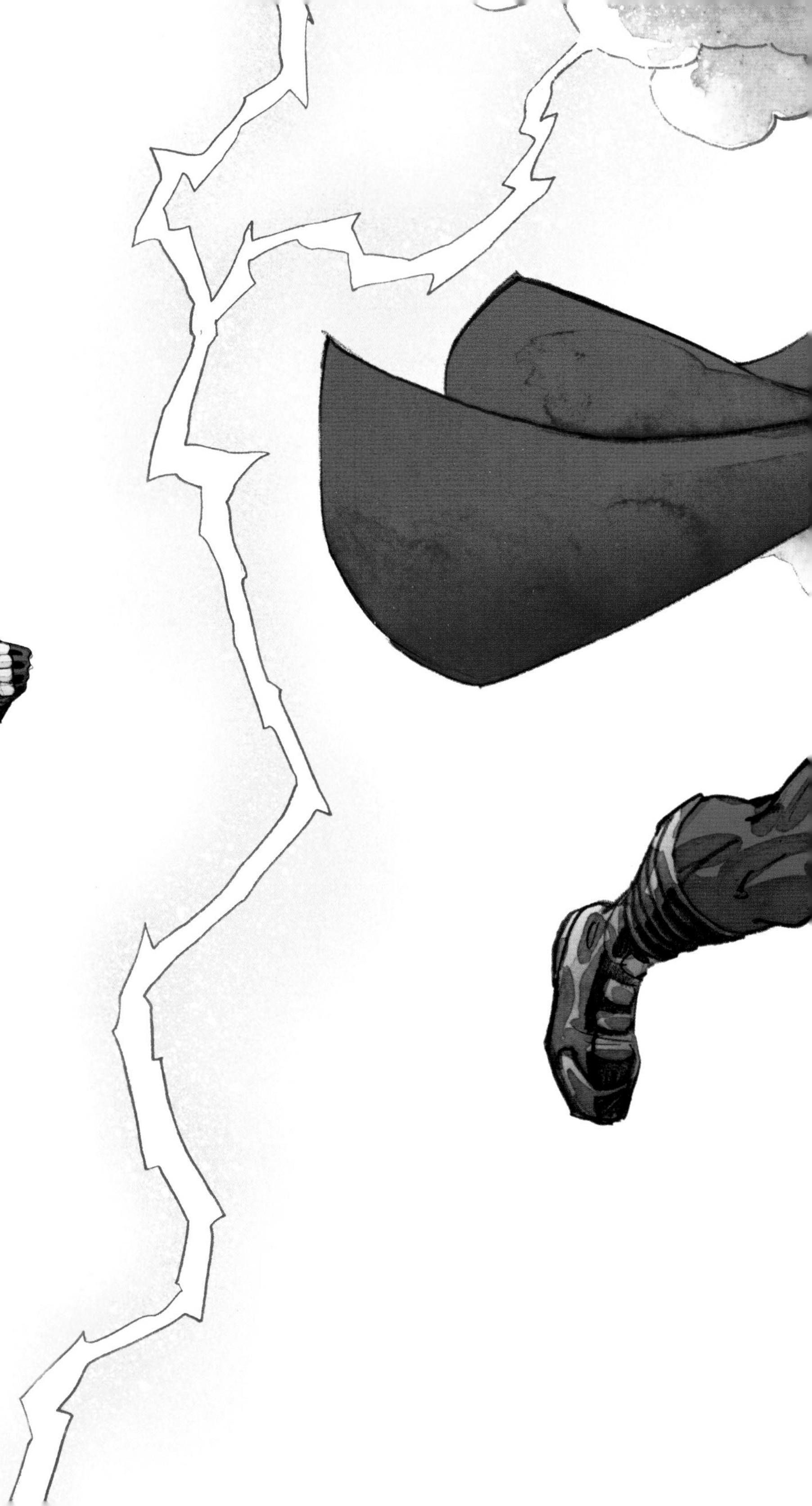

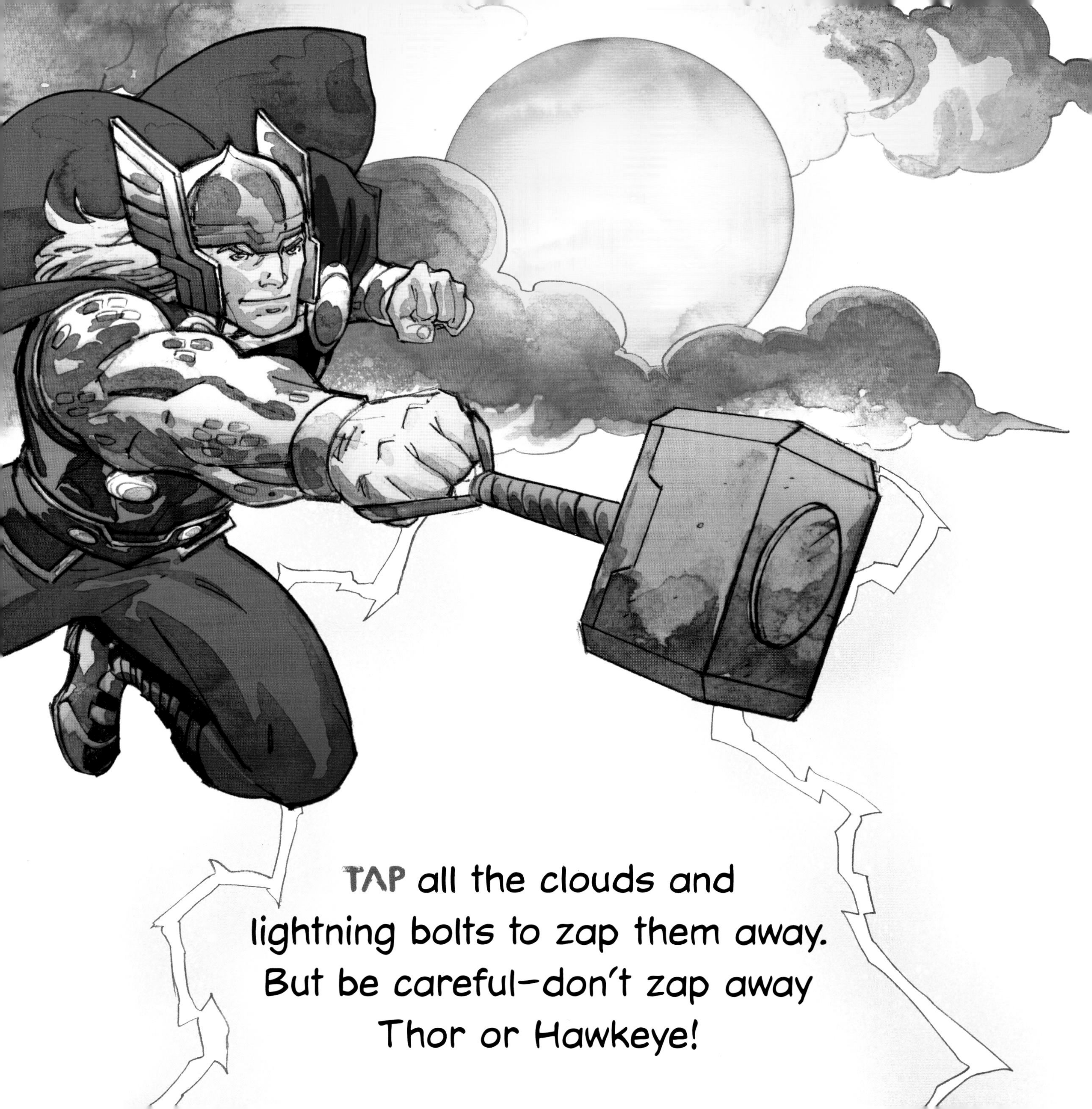

TAP all the clouds and
lightning bolts to zap them away.
But be careful—don't zap away
Thor or Hawkeye!

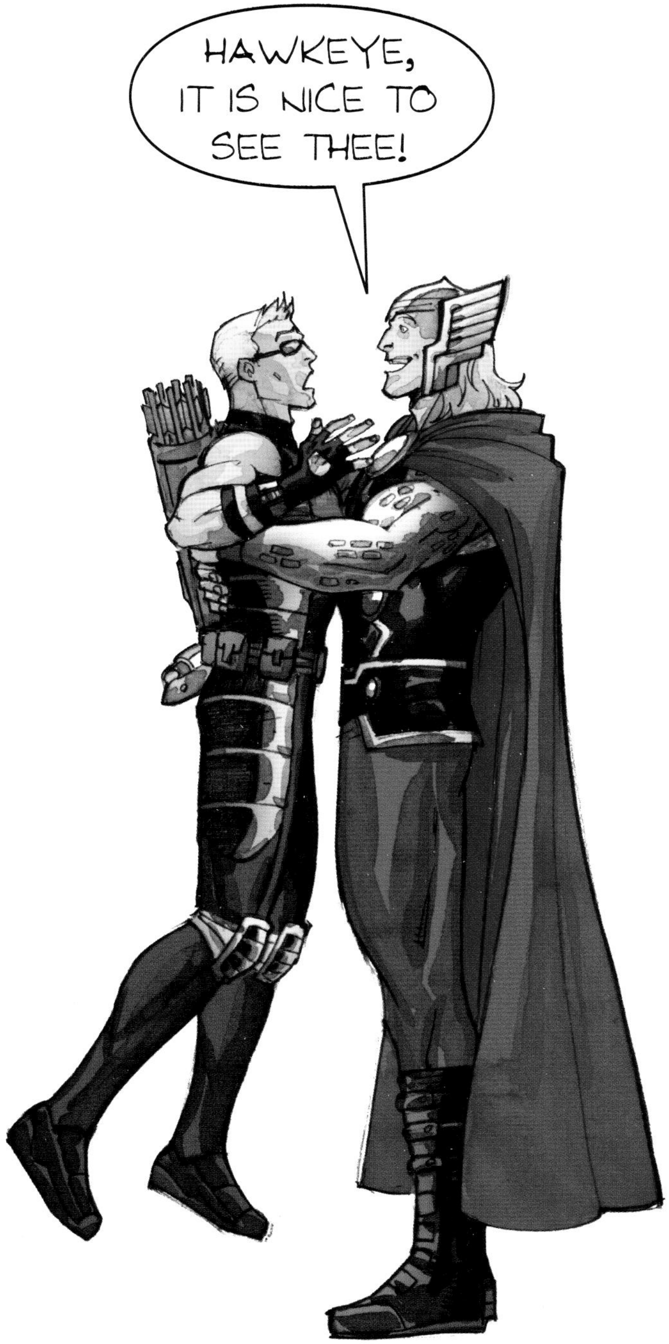
HAWKEYE, IT IS NICE TO SEE THEE!

LOOK! Is that
IRON MAN'S arc reactor?
PUSH it firmly
with your thumb
to find out!

Great job! Iron Man's here!
Now we have three Avengers!
Only four more to go.

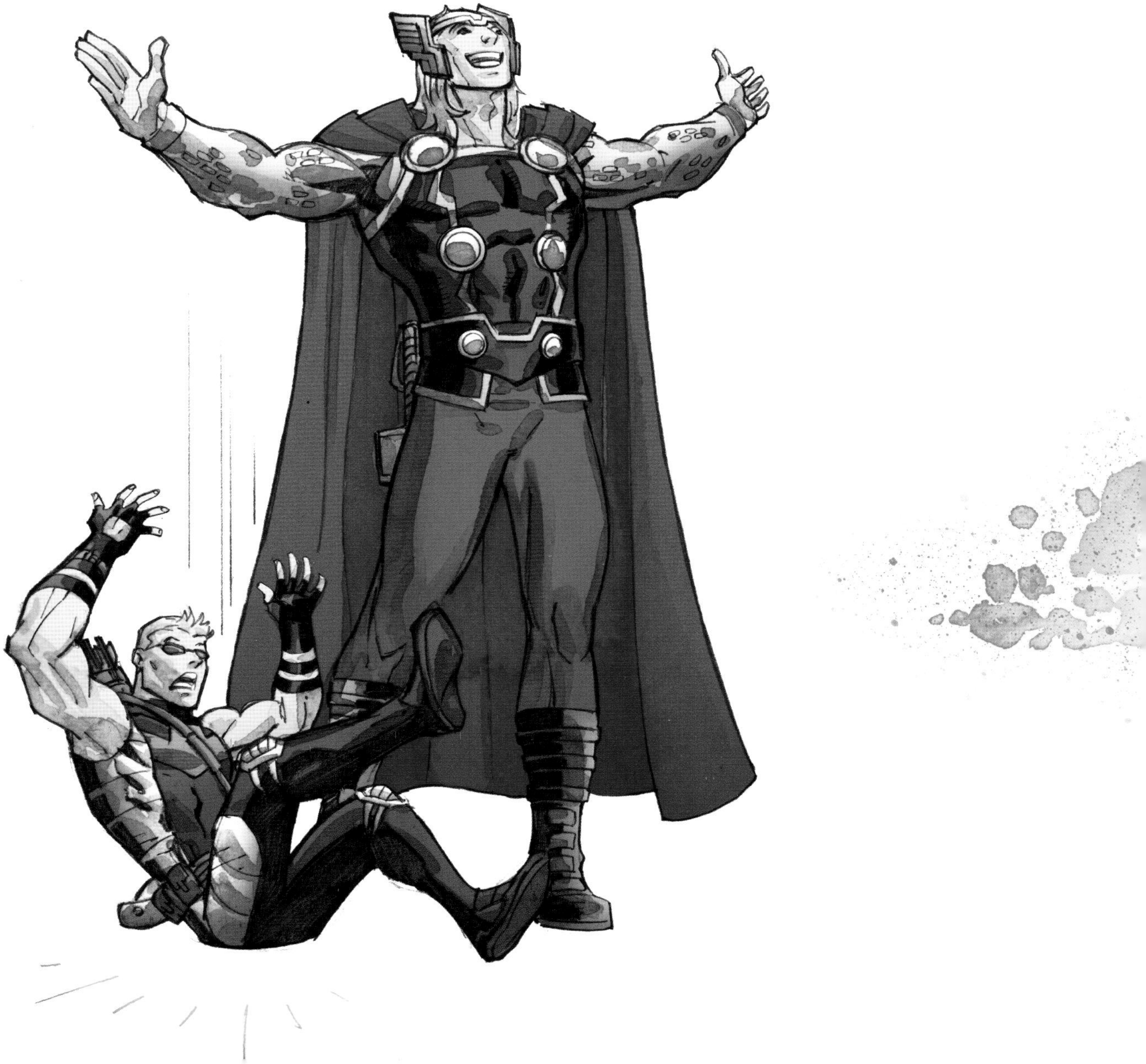

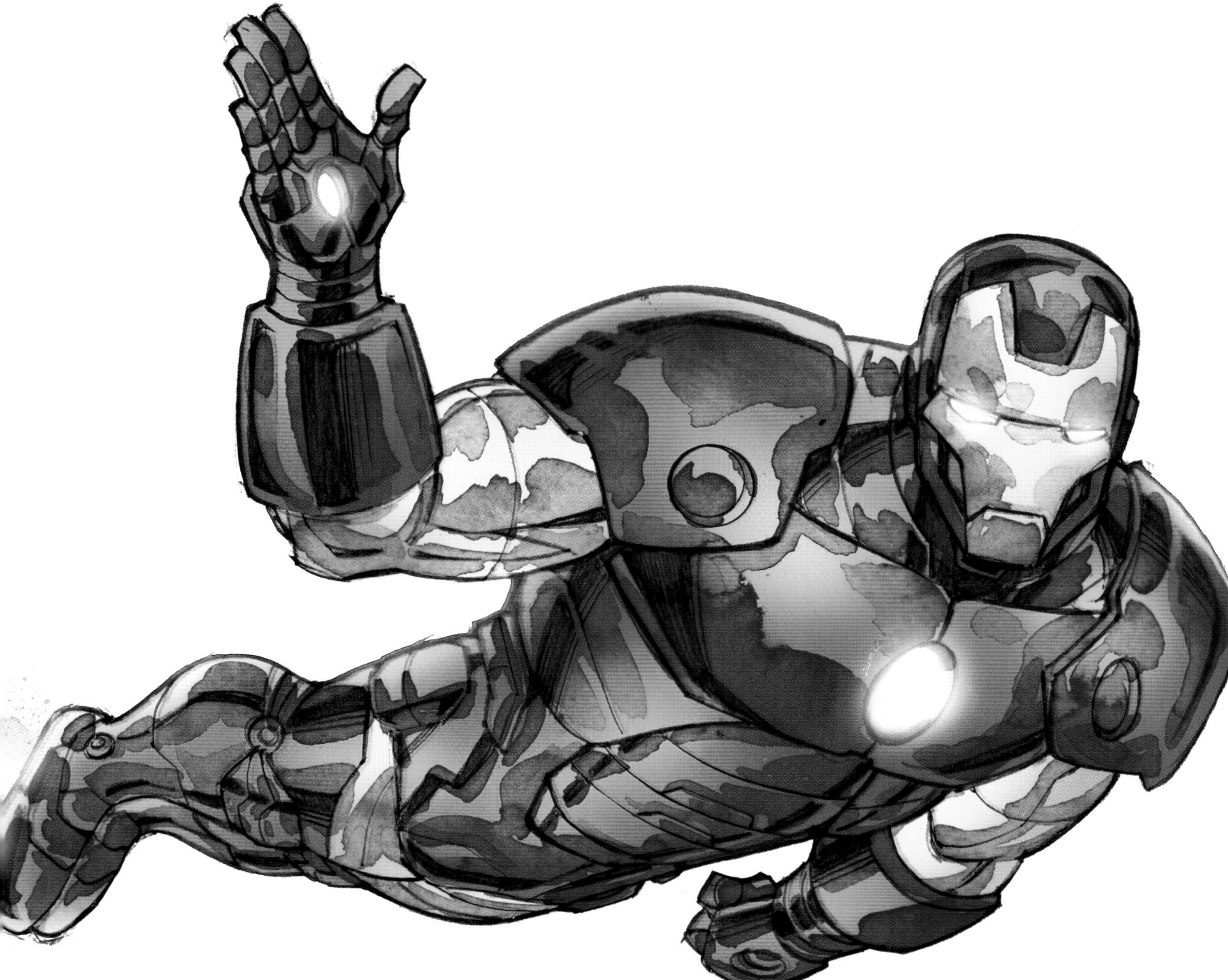

BLOW on the page
as hard as [illegible] can.

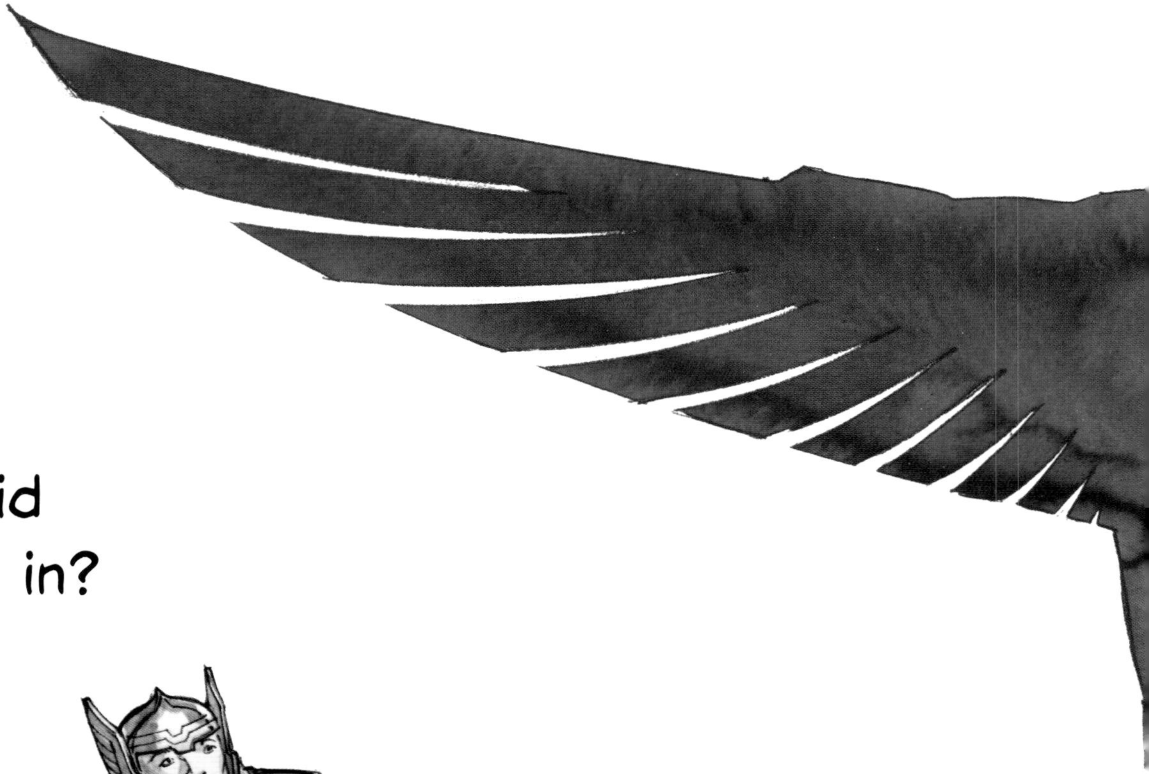

Now what did
the wind bring in?

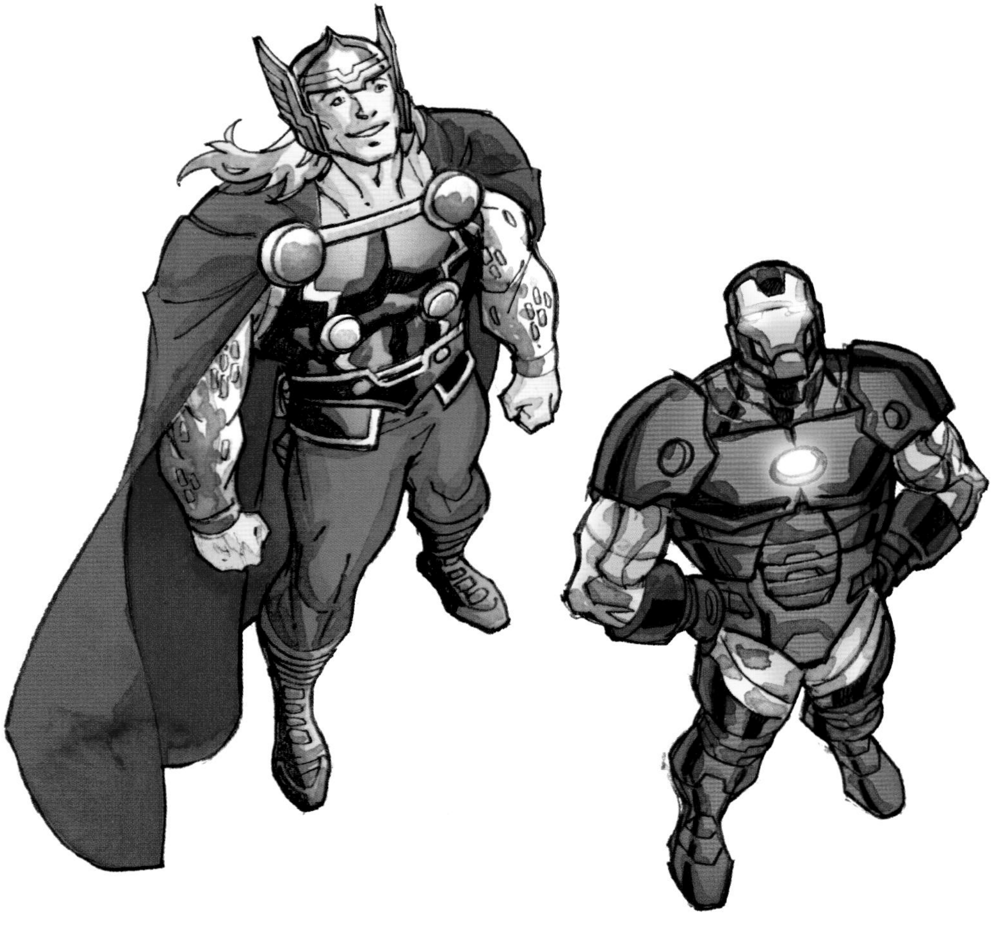

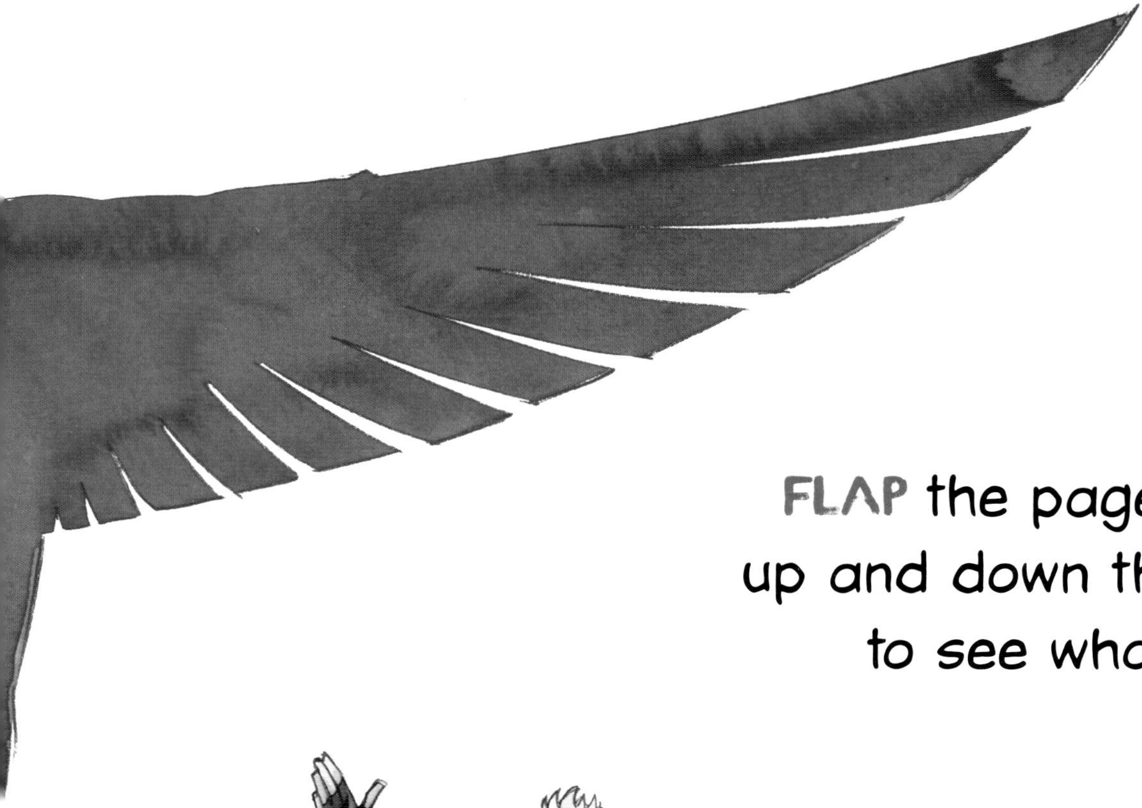

FLAP the pages gently up and down three times to see who it is!

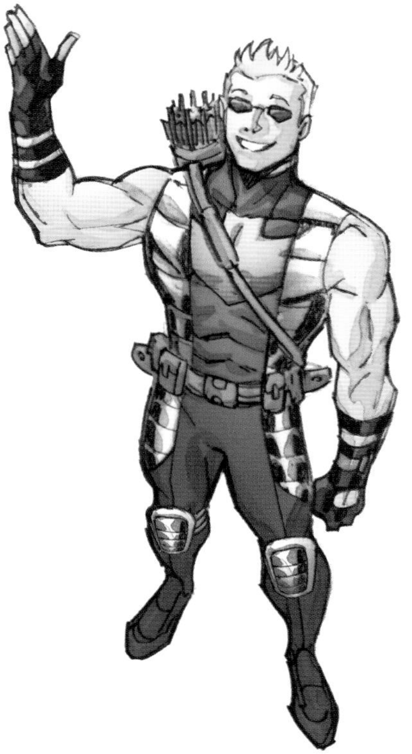

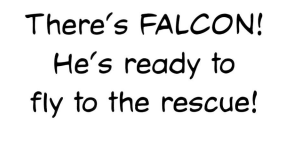

There's FALCON!
He's ready to
fly to the rescue!

LET
ME SEE
THAT.

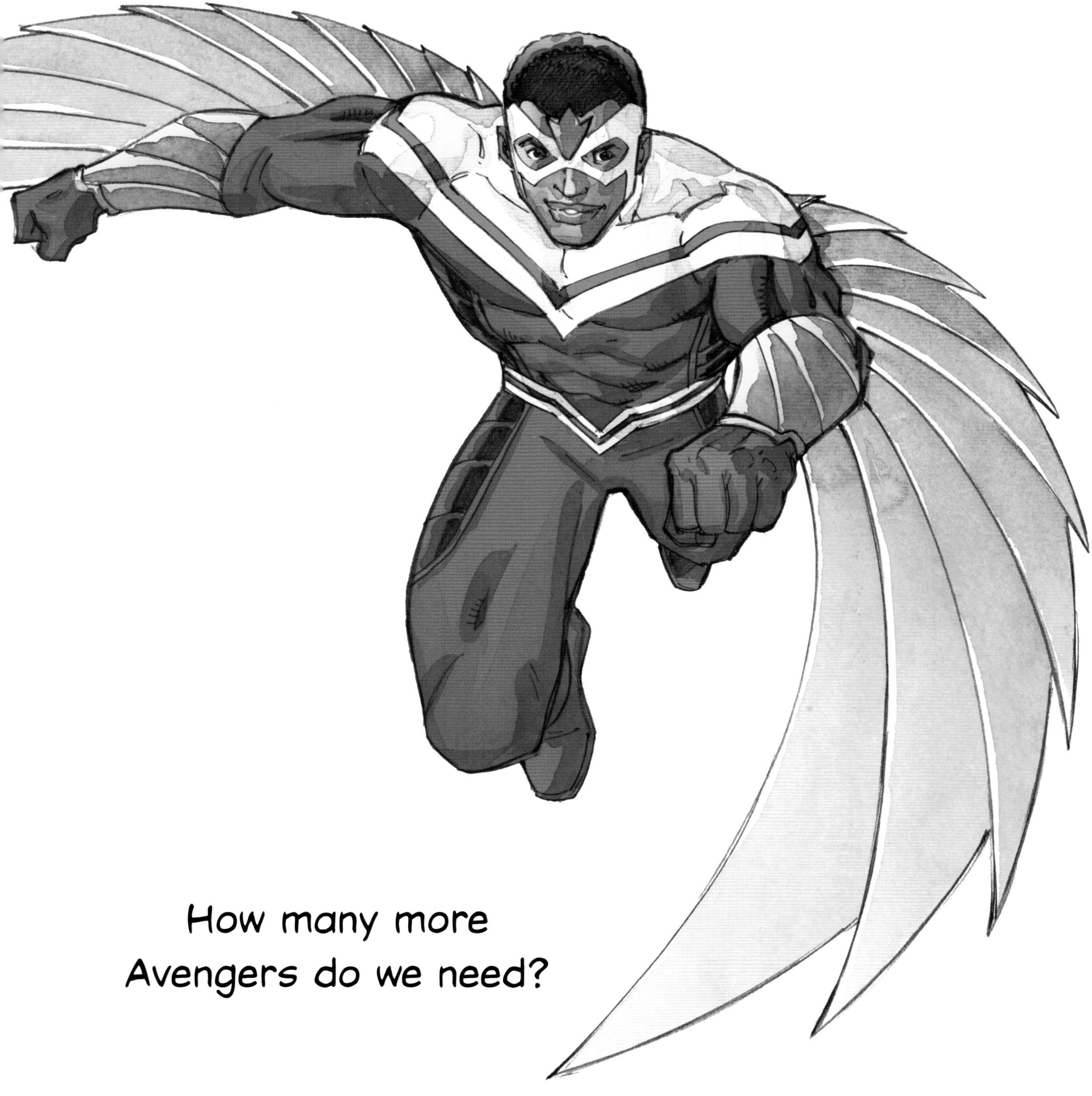

How many more
Avengers do we need?

Let's find BLACK WIDOW next. She would never let Iron Man get away with this kind of silliness.

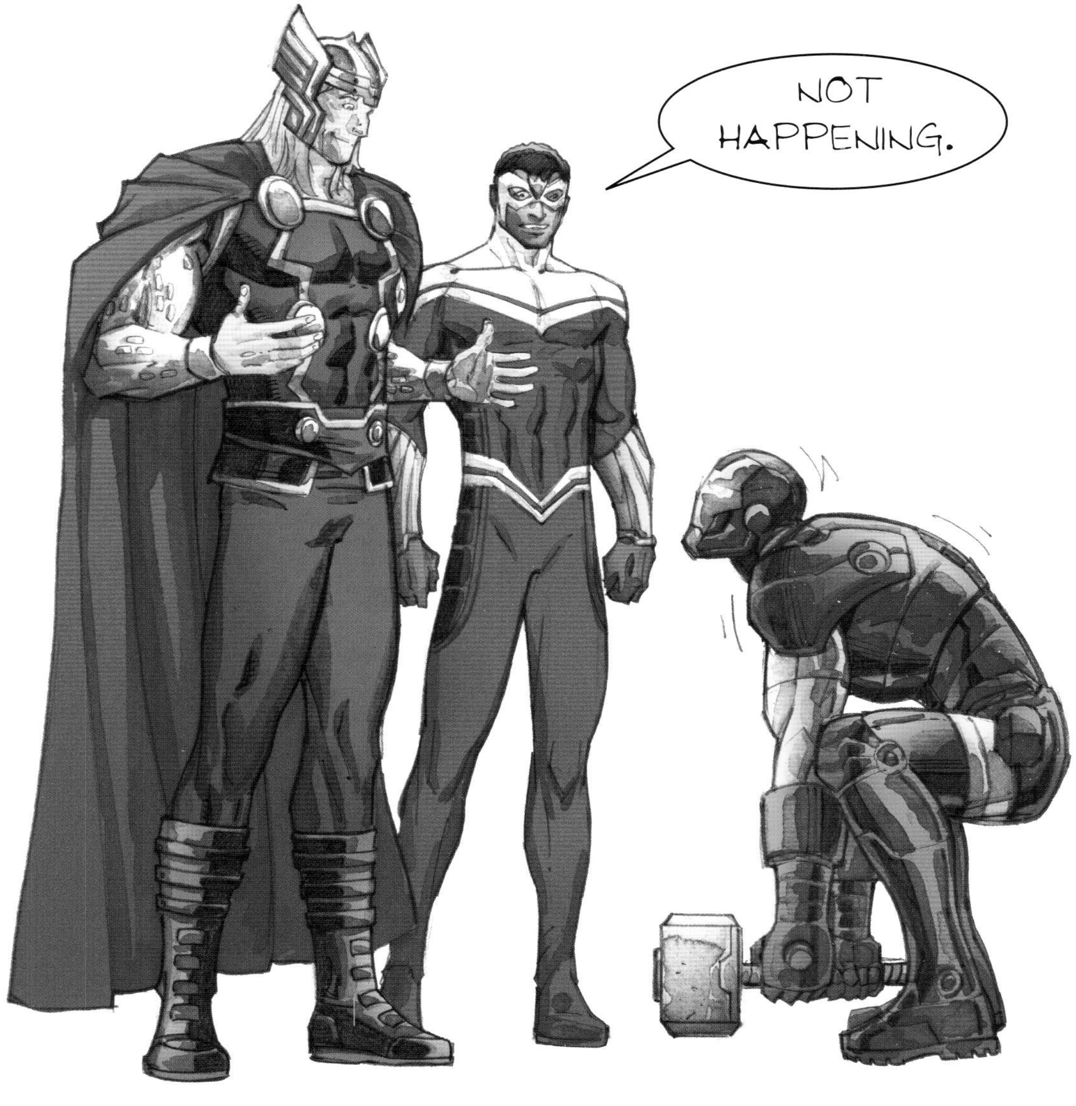
NOT HAPPENING.

Black Widow is a master of disguise.
She can hide in plain sight.
SWIPE your hand back and forth
across the entire page
to find Black Widow.

Whoa!

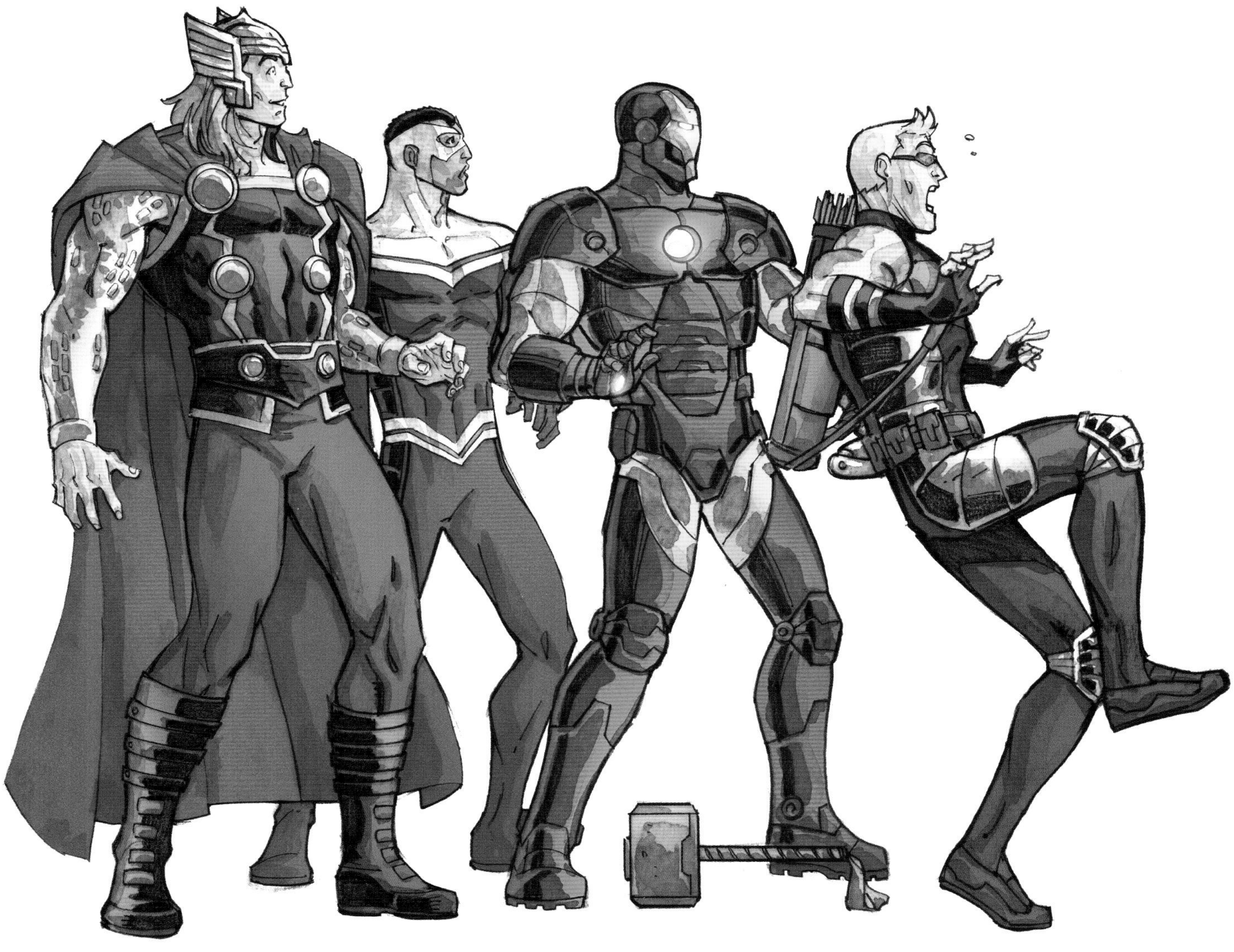

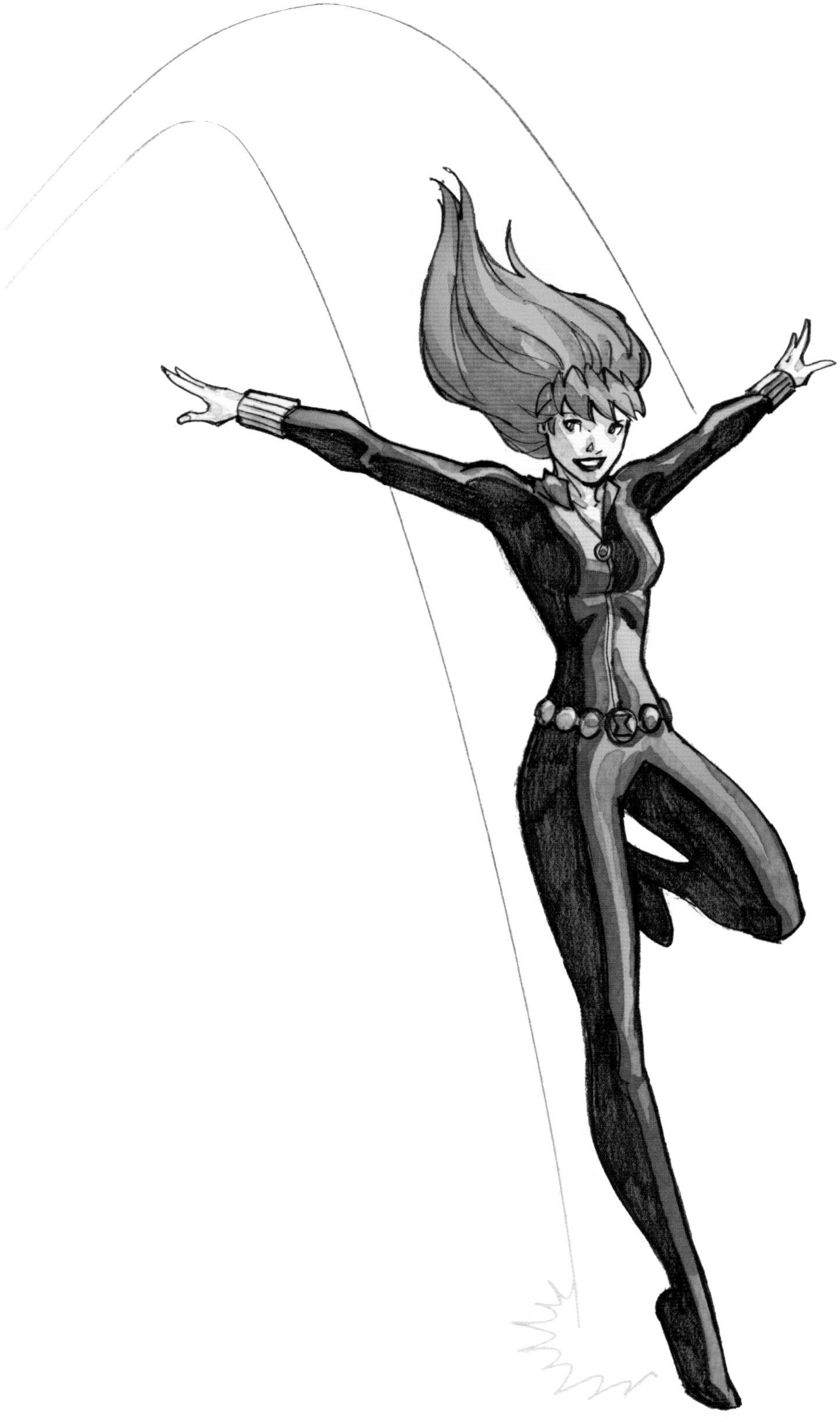

Black Widow
was here all along!

CAPTAIN AMERICA is next!

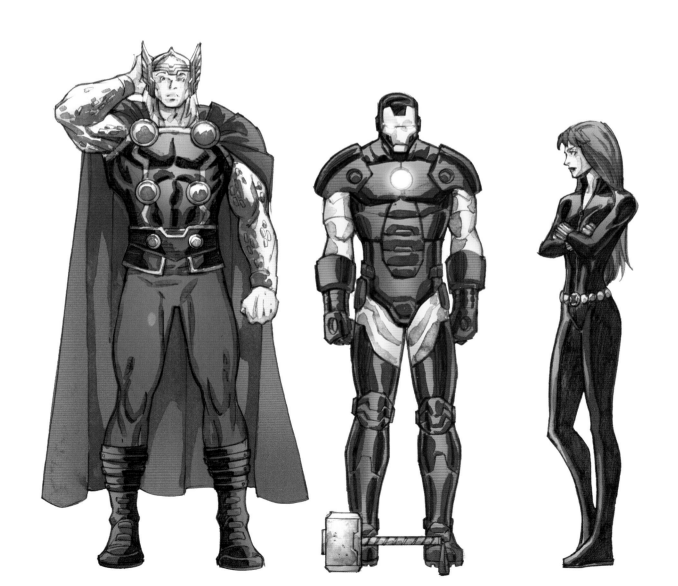

Hawkeye and Falcon
have his shield.
Give it a good strong FLICK
with your pointer finger
and see what happens.

Give a salute to Captain America!

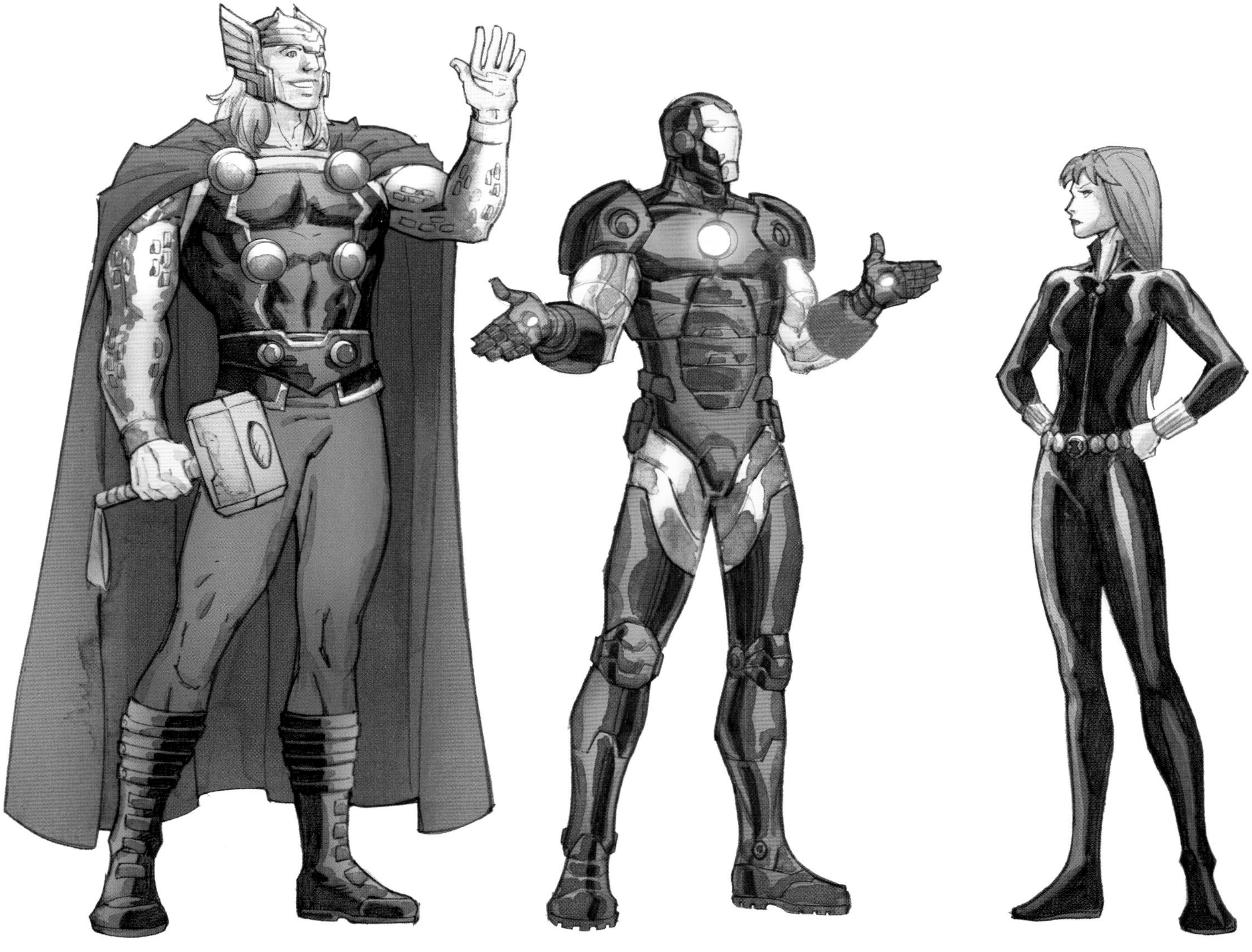

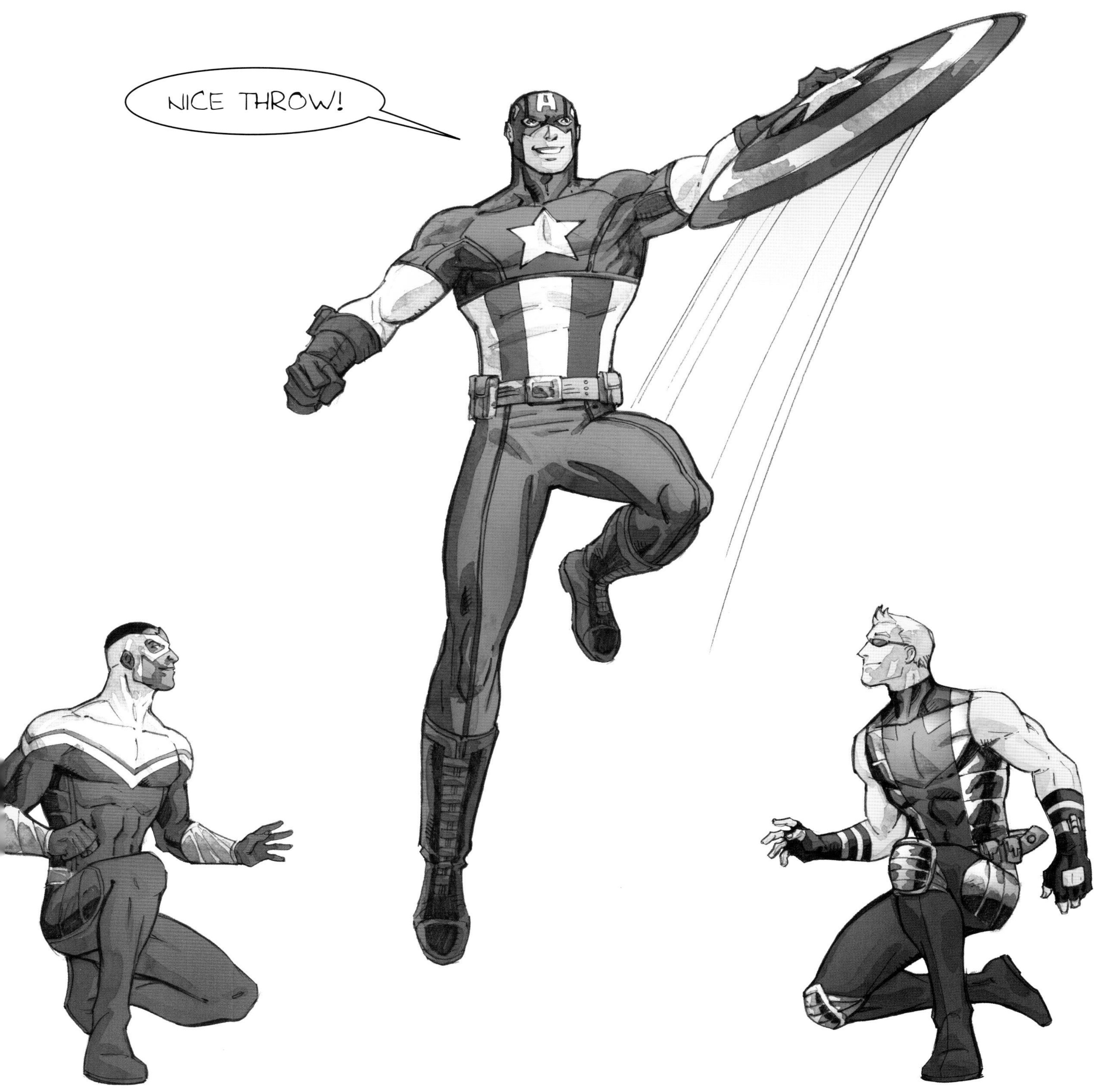
NICE THROW!

Cool!
All seven Avengers are assembled!
COUNT them as you give each one
a high five!

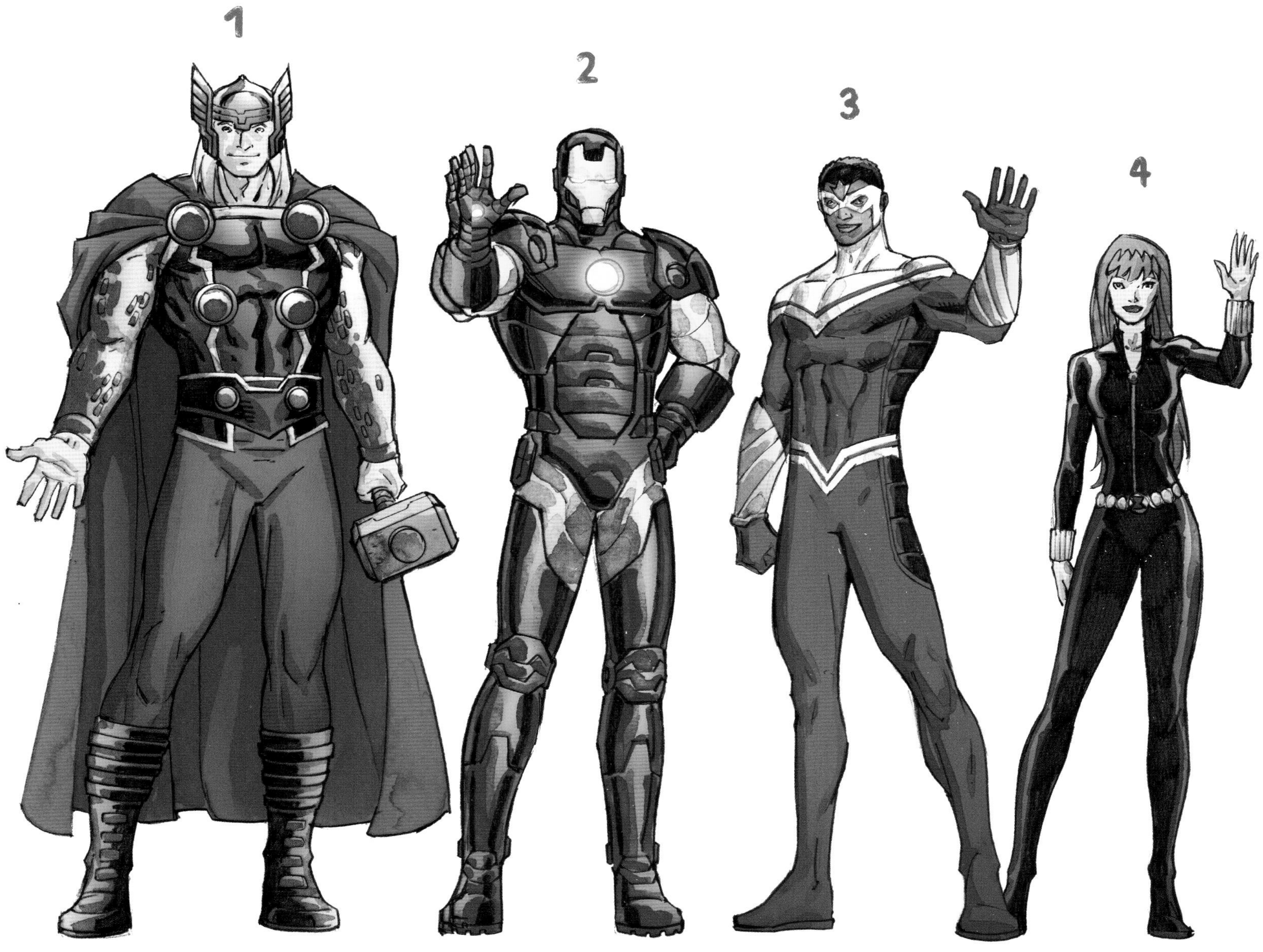
1
2
3
4

5

6

What's that?
There are only
~~SIX~~ Avengers here?
OOPS!
Who is missing?

That's right!
We still need the biggest
Avenger of all!

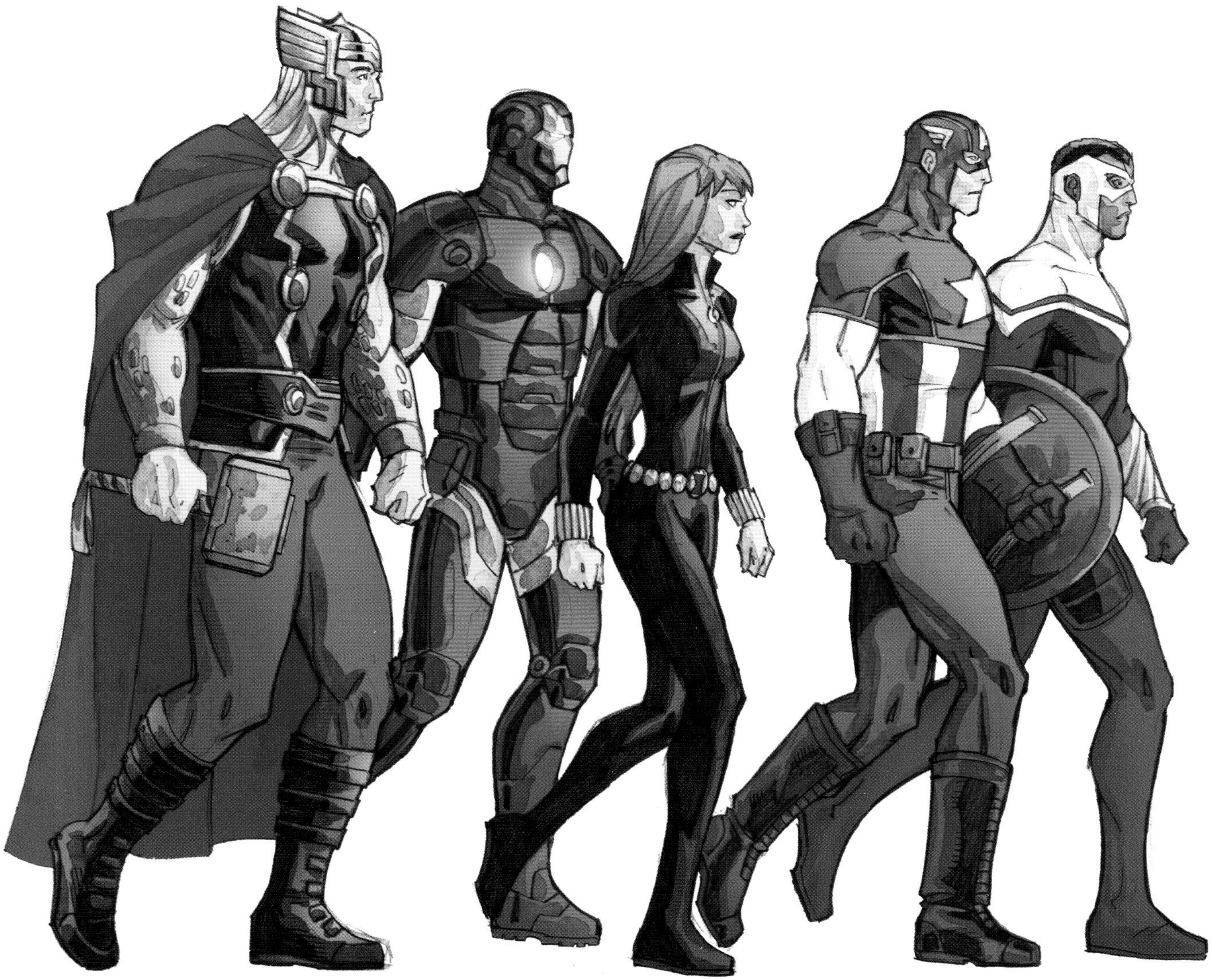

KNOCK three times
on this door.

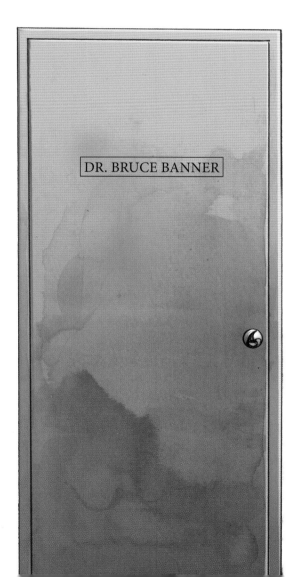

DR. BRUCE BANNER

There's Bruce Banner.
But we need the HULK.
The Incredible Hulk comes out
when Bruce Banner gets mad.

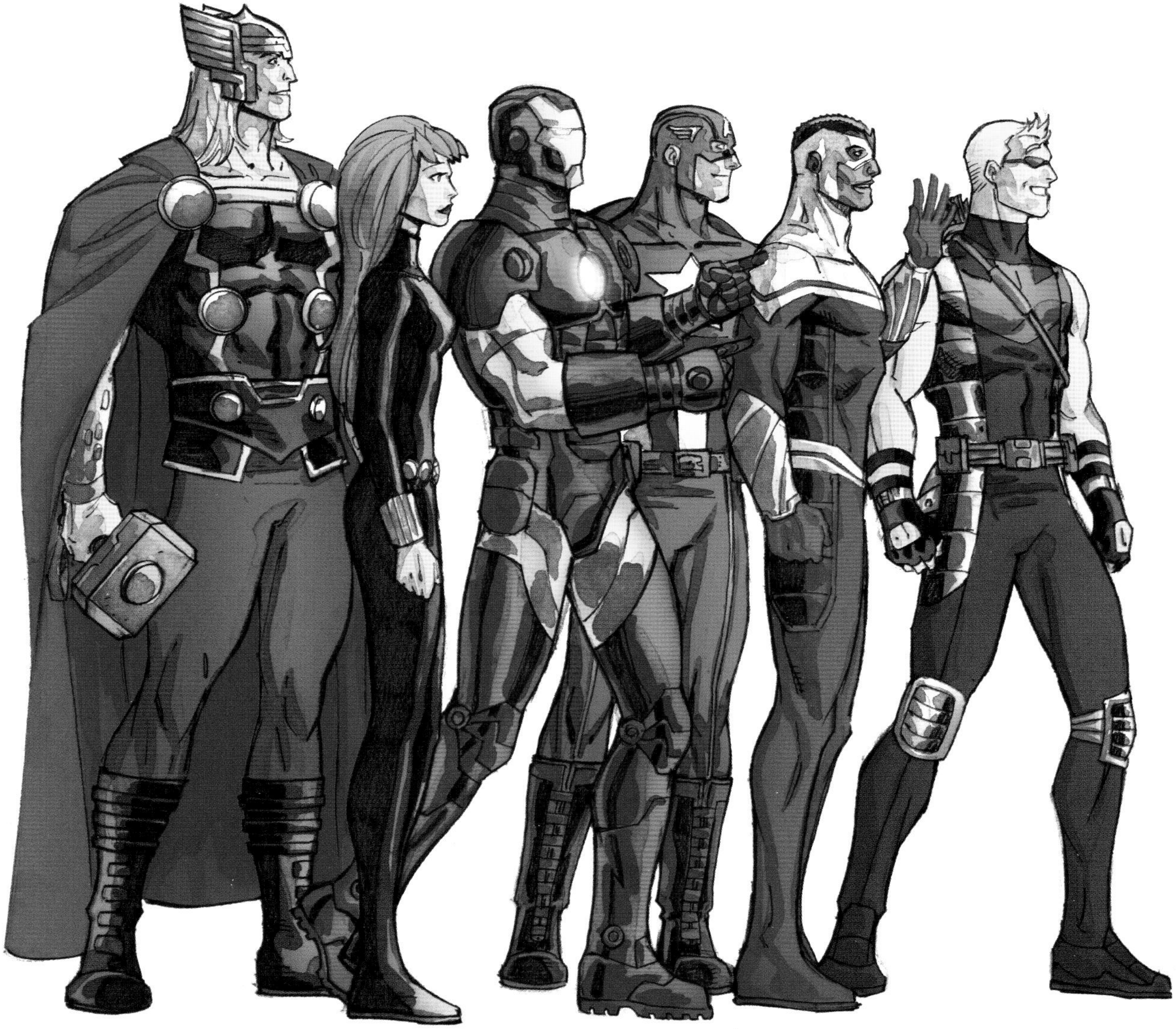

POKE Bruce Banner.

Good job!
He looks annoyed!

But he's not green yet.
TICKLE his tummy.
I bet he hates that.

Great!
He's getting mad!
But not mad enough.

SHAKE the book
up and down five times—
hard.

Don't give up!
You've got to get
the Hulk to come out!

This time give him your most
Hulkish ROAR. I dare you!

Well, that certainly
did the trick. . . .

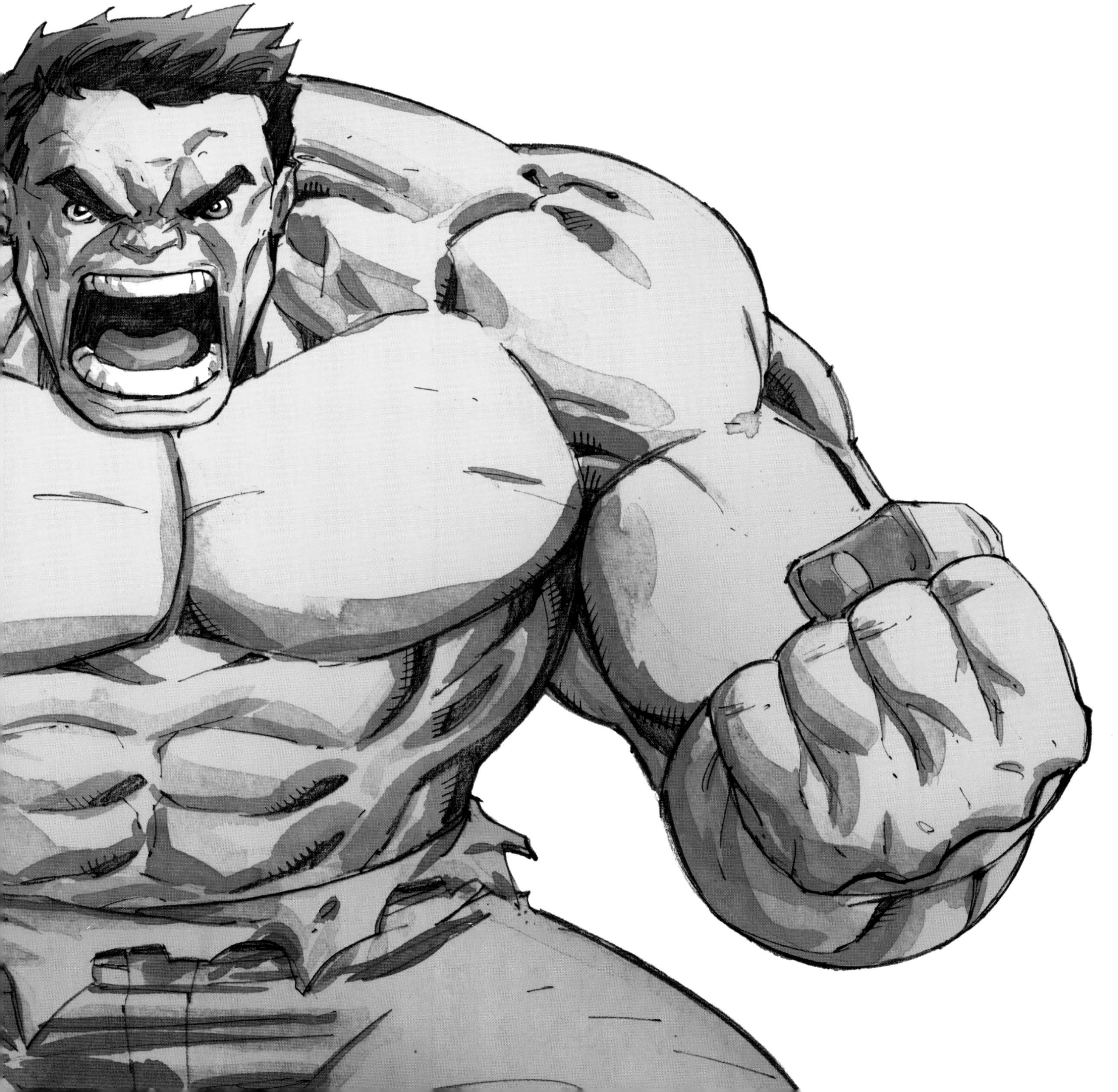

Hmmm.
Maybe we should calm
the Hulk down a little.

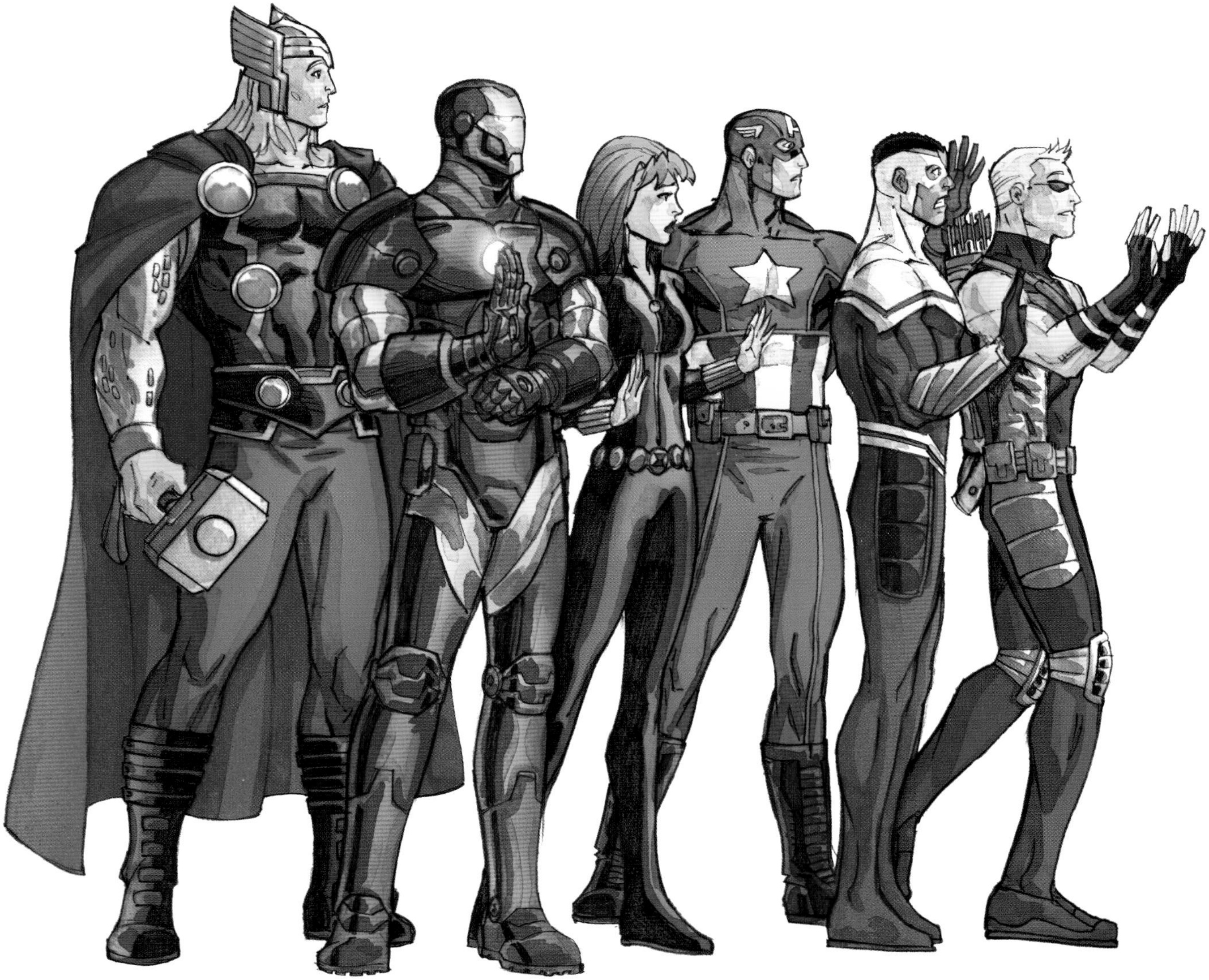

Give him a PAT on the shoulder.
There, there, Hulk. It's okay.

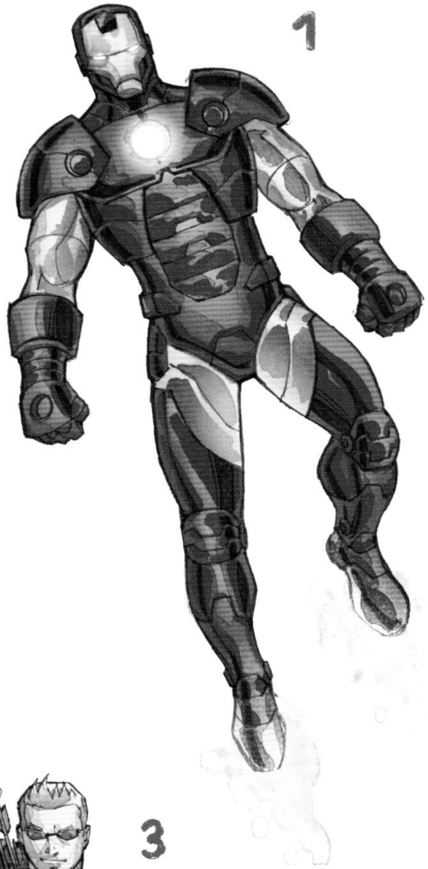

1

Now we're ready!
Let's
COUNT AGAIN.

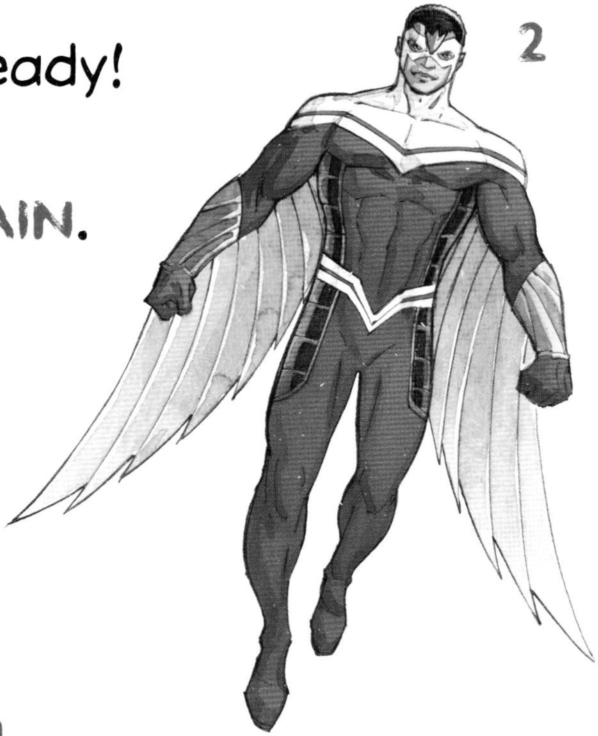

2

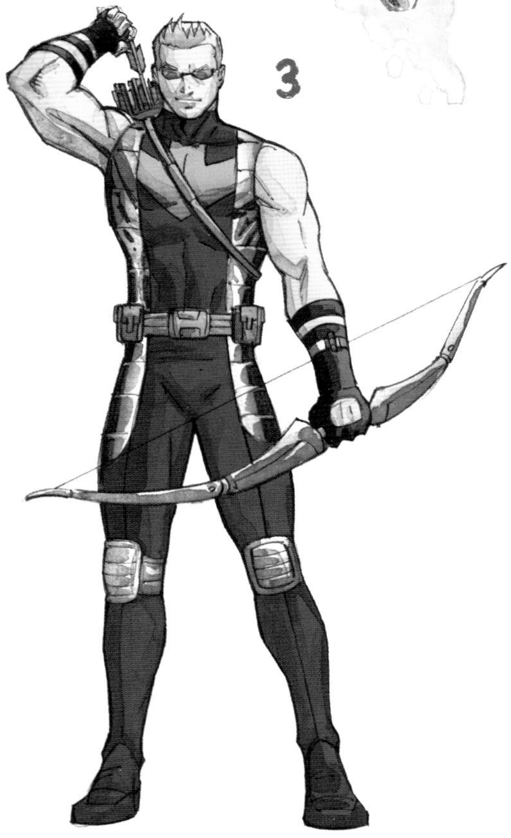

3

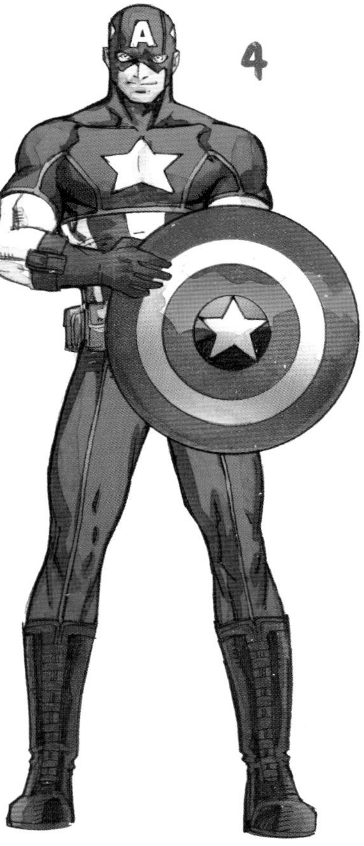

4

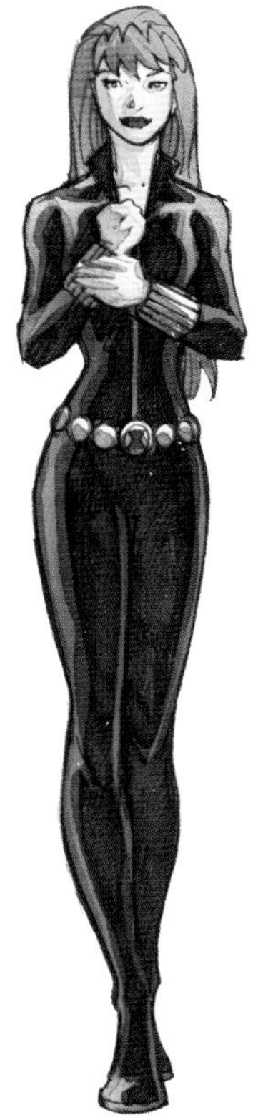

5

That's everyone! Now what?
Help the Avengers
remember their mission!
CLAP and **CHEER**
as loud as you can!

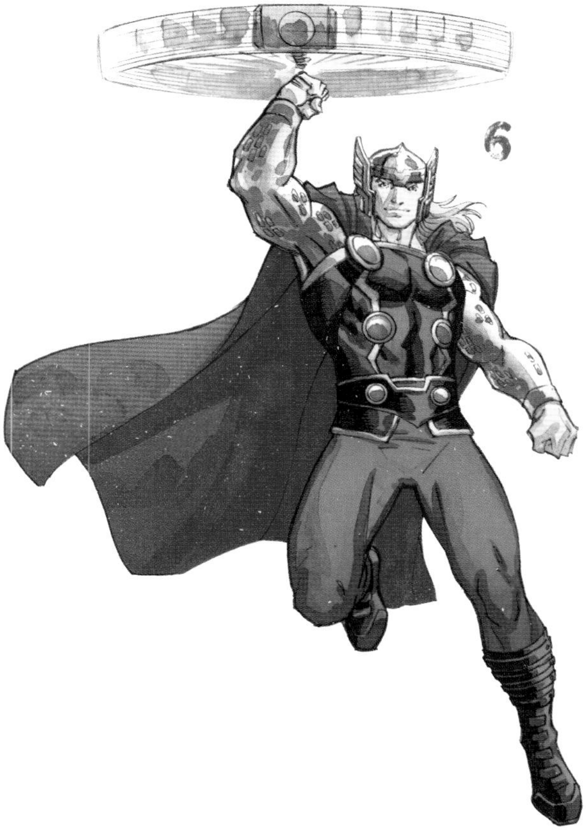

6

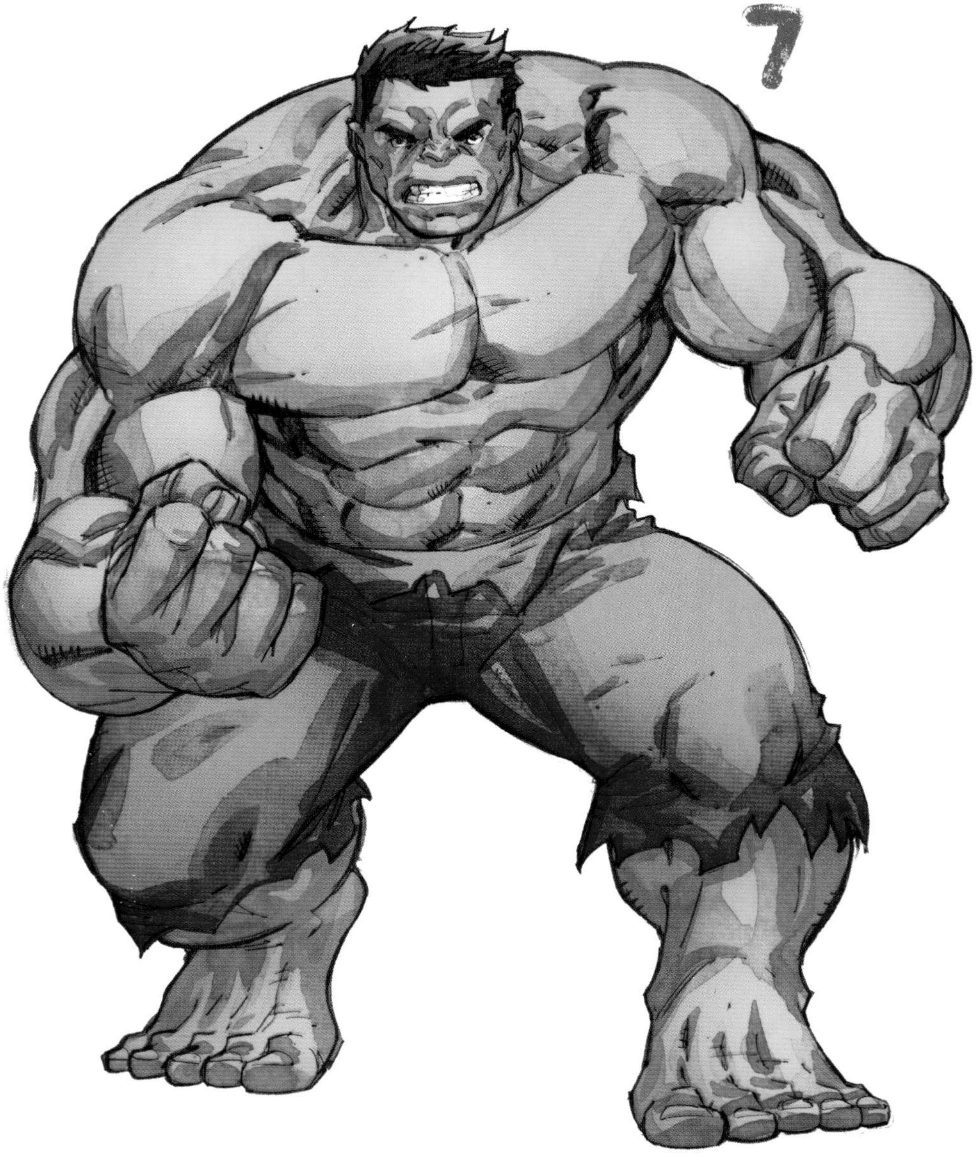

7

Oh, yeah!

AVENGERS, ASSEMBLE!

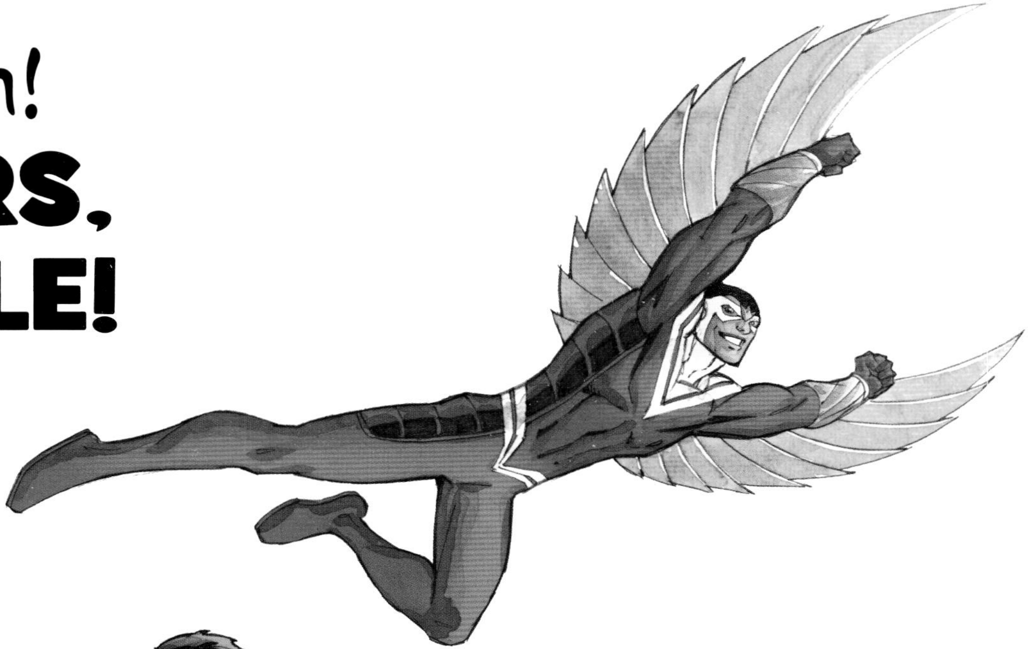

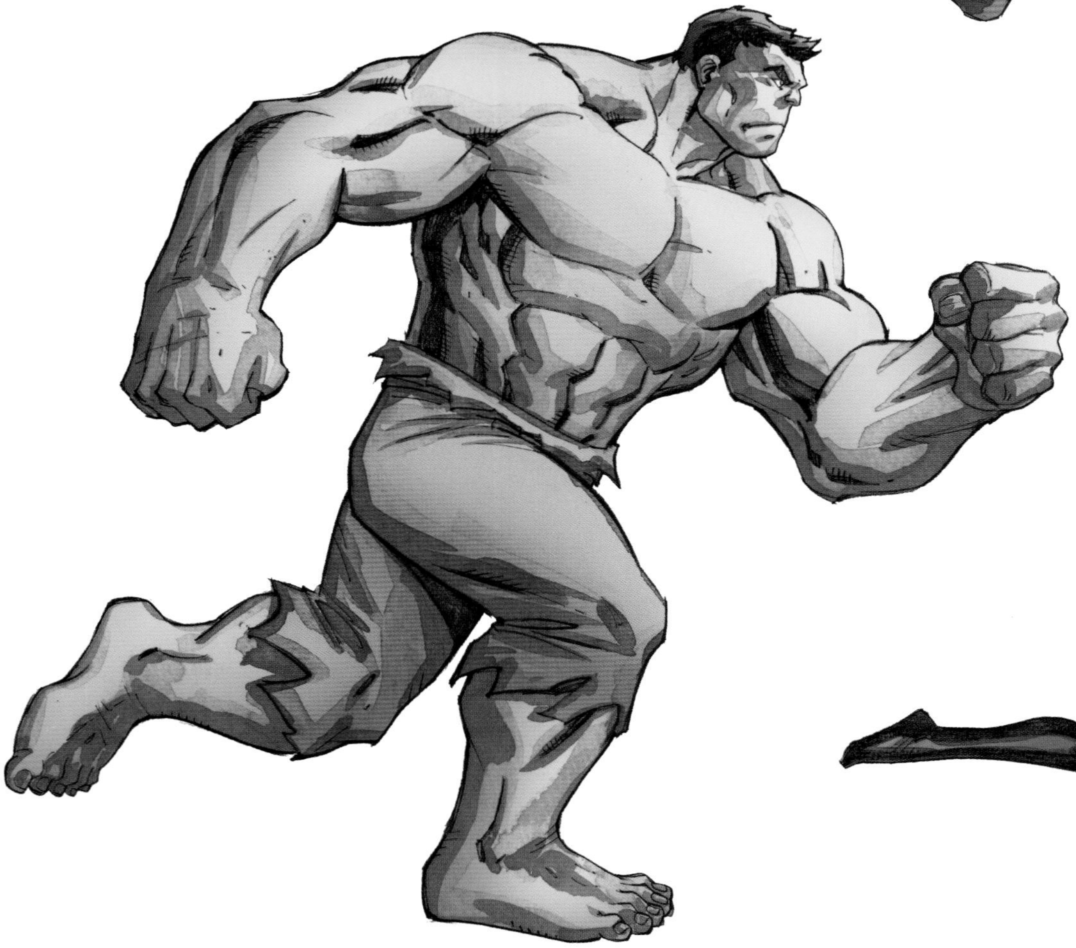

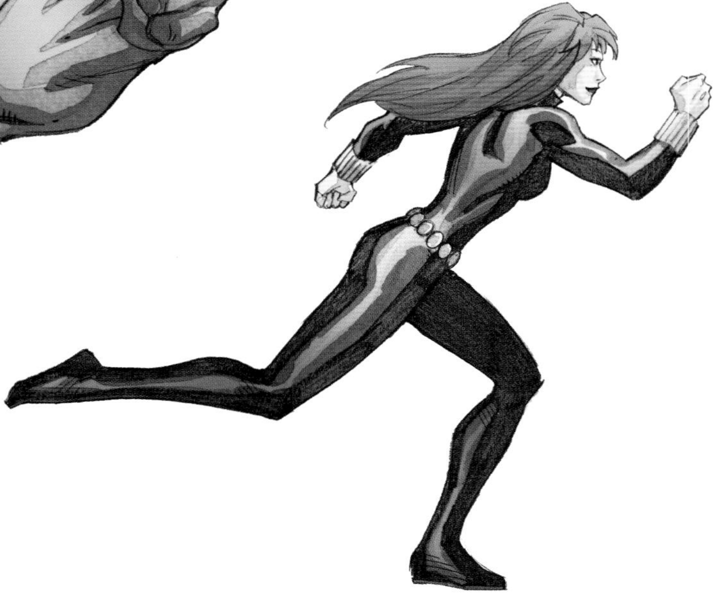

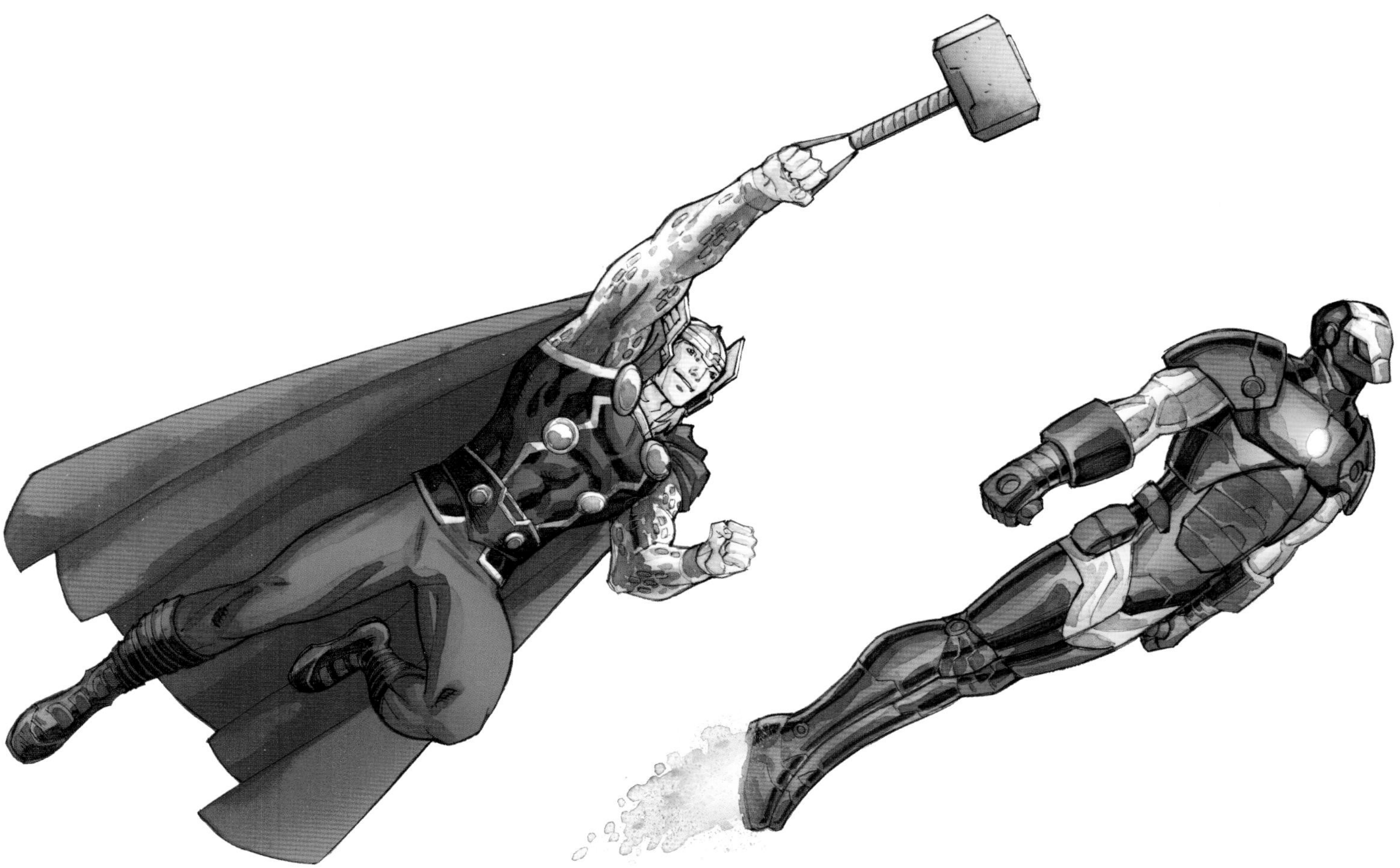
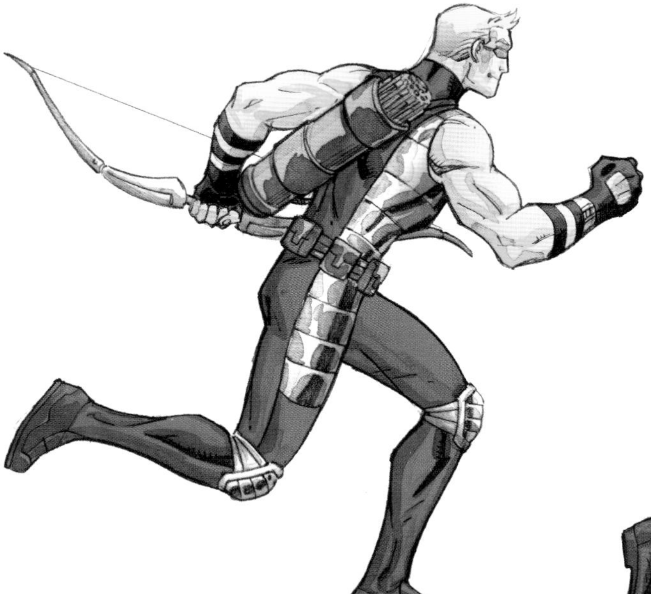
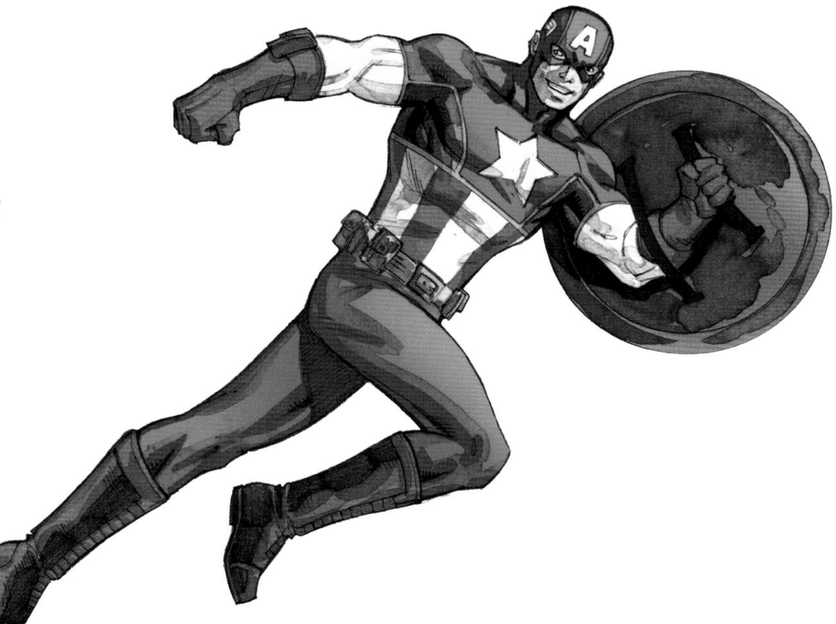

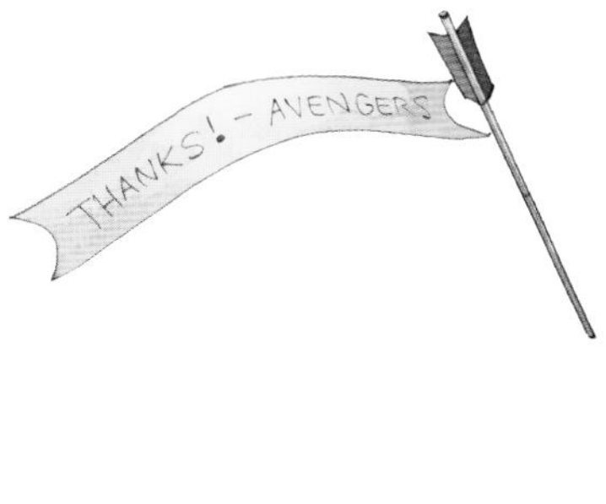
THANKS! - AVENGERS

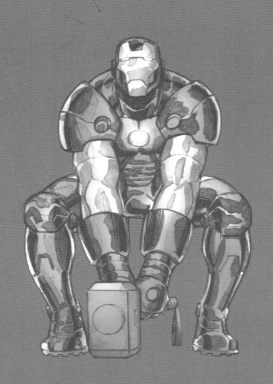